EL

MW00758056

By Janny Bonhomme

MILLCITYPRESS

Mill City Press, Inc.
2301 Lucien Way #415
Maitland, FL 32751
407.339.4217
www.millcitypress.net

Printed in the United States of America.

ISBN-9781072416418

Dedication

This book is dedicated with love, heartbreak, death and affection. To all those women, who suffered or had a tough time overcoming the troubles but now can get up and overcome it. This is for you, all the women who are stronger than ever to talk about what they've been through. To all the women, who have done a whole transformation of themselves who can now smile in joy and just be around positivity.

To all my women, here we stand

My children who inspired me and make me so proud.

They keep me going every single day.

~Robert,Tyshawn&Aiden~

My parents who raised me into the beautiful young lady I am today. They never left my side at all, was always there for me through good times and bad times; I can always count on them.

~Augusta&Jean~

My sisters and brothers who always motivate me and are by my side at all times. Up with me and rereading my book to make sure everything looks and sounds right. Dealing with my vexation. My biggest support team ever.

~Rebecca, Tatiana, Beatrice, laititia, Jr & Coby~

Last but not least my friends who motivate me all the time and push me to doing what I have to do. Always making sure, I am on top of my game and remain focus .Sisters for life

~Tameka, Makeda, Sharaine, Tenaya, Nnecka, Krystal, Trudy, GB and Tamar~

My parents had eight children. I had five sisters and two brothers but growing up with them wasn't easy. It may seem like it's not a big deal or anything, but having a big family we always had to share everything, like toys, the TV, etc. was I stressing over that? But it was annoying because

I would never have privacy and I couldn't wear the same clothes the kids in my school wore, such as name brands or have the latest phone.

One thing I must say about my parents is that they worked a lot and made sure we had a roof over our heads, food was always in the fridge, clothes on our back and for sure we were all doing well in school. I could never say my parents didn't show us love as kids. My parents weren't the type to say the words, "I love you." I guess it's a

Caribbean thing, because their actions always showed us they did and made us feel secured. I always wondered
why they weren't open like other parents that will say, "I love you," to their kids every day, but I never questioned it.

Maybe that's the reason why I am who I am today. Maybe that's why I am so cold–hearted. Maybe that's why I have so much anger. I am not blaming my parents; these are just questions I can't answer at this moment. Hopefully I will have answers soon.

My parents always looked out for me, especially when it came to my son. That was all that mattered. If I chose to finish school, I knew my mother would love that so much.

I got pregnant at an early age, and it was the scariest thing I ever had to experience. I found out at five months with no signs of anything, and then delivered at seven months. Yes, a lot of people had a lot of questions to ask, like, "How come you didn't know?" Let's just say the women's body is a scary thing. My menstrual was completely normal and I was eating more, but never thought I was pregnant. The crazy part of it all was there was a baby inside of me, growing, while I was running up and down the stairs in school and fighting nonstop. Now that I think about it, it probably was showing me that I needed to slow down because I was wild growing up. If I didn't get pregnant, I probably would have been in jail. Who knows? The way I was fighting back then, not even my mother could have stopped me.

I was bullied in elementary school and that feeling was not cool at all and I do not wish that on anybody's kids. There were days I didn't want to attend school because kids at my school put me through hell. They were picking on me every day until the day when I thought I was going to lose my eye from them throwing ice balls at me. I went after those girls one by one. After the first fight, I started making friends. The same girls that didn't like me wanted to be my friends. Crazy, right? Ask me if I care. Nope, you guys did not like me, so keep the same energy. My favorite line I tell everyone who never liked me or who thought I have a crazy attitude is, "I was not put on earth for you to dislike me point blank."

I really did not care who liked or disliked me at that point. My head was too hot, and I was ready for everything and anything. That is how my mind was set. Especially once I was pregnant at a young age, I lost a lot friends. The same friends

I was roaming the streets with, fighting with when they had beef, were same ones I lost because their parents did not want them to end up like me. As if their parents knew that their child was any better, but hey, who am I to judge and tell? Not my cup of tea. "Life goes on," is how I see it.

I was home schooled. I cried so many nights until I gave birth. I even wanted to get an abortion, but it was way too late or not safe. I thought my life was over: no more hanging out with my friends, no more roaming the streets after school. Everything changed. I guess I can also thank God for my pregnancy. I did a whole 360 and changed my life, because now I had a little one I must take care of. I blocked a lot of people out of my life. My main focus was to finish school and find a job. If it

wasn't for my mom, I probably would have never finished school.

I was going to school and right after was working. It was very hard and tiring, but I had to do it. There were so many times I wanted to give up, but my mom was not one for the excuses.

"If you were doing what I sent you to do, none of this would've happened at all," she said. She was right, and I had to stand up and accept that I was a

young mother.

I appreciate my parents so much. They could have turned their backs on me like some parents do, but they are the ones who helped me reach so far today. Of course, I had my ups and downs, but who doesn't?

Yes, I finished school. I calmed down a lot for the sake of my son. I had to be a better person. This could have happen to anyone, whether you are alone or have someone that can help you, and I am glad I had my parents. Even if you're alone, don't stop doing what you have to do. You can't always depend on someone to fix your problems that you put yourself through. You will have some who are willing to help you down the road, but who knows what the outcome will look like? Everyone goes through something, maybe something like you, so don't think it's the end of the world.

I spent a lot of sleepless nights studying and working four hours, five days a week. It was too much for me, but I did it to myself. There were no excuses, though. You thought my mom was going to take my responsibilities? Nope. Did she send me to go have sex at a young age? Nope. She helped me a lot in the best way she could, and my sisters, too. With God, my family, and my few friends to help, I was all right.

Being a young mother opened my eyes. I was young, so not everyone knew I had a kid, so I felt like I could still run the streets and hang out with friends, do normal things kids my age were doing. My childhood changed and I didn't like it one bit. I was hearing my friends were making new friends and I guess I felt jealous.

I was the youngest at my job, and before hearing their stories I thought I had it bad. The only thing I had to deal with was getting pregnant at a young age. I didn't stop doing what I had to do for myself or my son. I was getting stressed and mad at the world for What I did. I guess that's where I got my anger from. Who knows?

I still didn't have an answer for my questions. I was adding more to the list of unanswered questions. Next thing you know I was hanging with friends, but new friends. I started partying

two nights in a week to seven days a week. I was being a mom,
working and partying. At this point I guess I was being selfish, but I didn't care because I was having fun, the fun that I thought was stolen from me.

Have you ever heard the saying, "When you mess with fire, you get burned," or, "What makes you hot will make you cold"? You guys don't understand. I really thought I was living life. I was enjoying music, dancing and drinking. My life was so fun…Well, I thought it was. I was so relaxed. Going out every night was so much fun. It was like I had to two jobs but one at night, and I didn't get paid. Imagine doing that seven days a week, knowing I had other responsibilities, getting two to five hours of sleep each night.

I was enjoying myself, so sleep wasn't important. Those sleepiness nights were making my skin look old; I looked tired out. Now that I look back at it, I would rather be a mother over partying. I was young and doing stupid things, I

guess. I really paid $20 every night to party with people who were barely dancing and $10 for liquor, but then you see your enemy. Literally, I would do the same thing every night repeatedly. I should've saved that $30 and done something with my three sons or hung out
with girls instead of partying.

Or I could have continued to hustle on the side by doing peoples' hair. I enjoy doing that also. The only problem is I hate to be annoyed, so when I
get annoyed that is when I stop doing hair for a while. Once I am ready I do it again I love doing hair, but the people that you get can be so annoying at times. They run late, then they want to tell you step-by-step how they want their hair. *Okay, I get it. You want it to look good, and I want it to look good, too, because I want to build clientele. So why would I make your hair look crazy? So you can walk around and talk about me? Big no.*

I still want to open up my hair salon and have people work in it. It's still my dream and I am going to make sure it happens, too. This is how I feel now but what I did is done. You live and learn a lot of things in life. How I see it, you must experience things in life to say, "I've done that and is not for me at all." I pretty much tried out everything. Ask me if I will repeat some of those things. My answer will be, "No." I am getting older, not younger, and I am at the point in life where I do not have time for certain things in life anymore.

I know there were days that my mother wanted a day or two to relax, but I guess I took advantage. Before I would step my foot out the door she would say, "Take your kids with you, I can't talk today," or, "Talk to them before you leave." I was tired of hearing the same lines every day, so I started to stay home. I learned that the same thing we put our parents through, our kids are going to do the same but in a different format.

I had a lot of questions people would ask me on a daily basis, like, "How did you do the partying and everything?" In all honesty, my body just adjusted to it. It's like your body get used to getting up every day, So you cannot stay in bed for too long because making money is on your mind. That is how.

Like I said, being a young mother wasn't easy, but I wasn't going to walk around mad at the world for what I did. Yes, you get stressed out and feel like you can't do it anymore, but you can't let the stress take over your body and mind. It is safer to deal with your problems or let it out before letting
it out on someone you love or know. I did that a lot.

I would be so stressed here and there because I held everything in and take it out on anybody, not caring what came out my mouth. One thing I learned is when I am angry I stay to myself until I calm down. I would say the meanest thing ever and still be mad and hours later I would sit there and say to myself, "Did I just say all of that?" It took me a

while, and I am still working on it now.

Some days, I would explode. There are so many mean things you can say because you angry and I took out all my anger on people, not caring what came out or how it sounded. But I was mad at the time. I still feel bad to this day. I know I hurt a lot of people and I am sorry for that.

I just wanted to be at a peaceful point in my life, but I knew I had to fix my problems within myself to get to the point. A lot of that anger came from broken promises, a broken heart, being lied to, and people always putting their two cents in when they did not know what they were talking about deep down. It came from a lot of angles.

I was always so high-tempered, I never listened to anyone. When someone would talk with me for my own good, I would always think they are coming at me sideways. I didn't know how to take criticism well; I still don't. Well, that is something I must fix in myself.

Sometimes it is good to take good advice from someone, but at the same time when you have your guard up you are always alert to things. I guess that comes from broken promises and broken heart. I just do not trust anyone. How do you trust another when all you keep getting is a broken heart? All the trust you keep letting out over and over from start to end, end to start. At one point in life you are going to want to throw it out the window and say, "Forget it." Is it worth it? But you must start one way. You cannot always keep that same energy. Look who's talking. Me, the person who has trust issues, who always thinks someone is out to get me. Like I said, I am still working on myself and remaining positive. You're only overlooked, rejected and ignored by the people not meant to be in your life, period.

I started throwing parties. Money was good, so why not, right? But with all that money came the stress, the hate and people losing their lives that I thought that will be around forever. I couldn't continue being selfish anymore. I realized I had three boys to take care of. I wanted to be something in life, finish college, and get married someday.

I have a strong support team and so do my kids. Thank God for that. It was time for me to start thinking positive again and remember I was doing this for my boys, so they could have a better life then me. I helped people who were around me and God blessed me ten times more, so I am thankful for that.

I see people who party for a living, with no job or anything. They pop bottles every day and deep down they are broke. Let me know if I am wrong or not: Can you file taxes with partying? If so, I wish someone would have told me a long time ago because I lost so much money. I can't judge, though. I was once that girl who was throwing parties and going out seven days a week like it was paying my bills and feeding my kids.

Sometimes when you throw a party it is either a hit or a miss type of deal. You must take pictures with the promoters, or take one alone, buy a bottle and pass out your flyers to everyone. I had to do that every night. If you didn't attend someone's party, you lost someone out of your party. By me saying that I mean for example let's say today is someone party and your party is Saturday. If you miss today party they will not attend your party on Saturday. This was a lot of stress and a lot of lost money but once you learn from your mistakes, it won't happen again. I was spending too much money, and seeing the same people repeatedly was tiring.

In the party scene, it was like people just came to watch others and talk about them. I went out to have fun, but it was crazy. People really spent money to watch people. Like, am I paying your bills? I was making my own money and paying my own bills so I could do what I wanted. The same goes for anyone who's doing the same: Do what makes you happy. I believe people should be leaders, not followers. Don't let anyone take away that joy of yours.

I let someone take my joy away. I was in love… Well, I thought I was. I was so blind to everything until I looked at myself in the mirror and asked,

"What are you doing? You need to put your feet down and get it together a.s.a.p." I was called fat and ugly, and was told that no one was going to want me with three kids. I was cursed out with every curse word in the book. Why? Because I didn't want to go by his rules anymore. Why should I when he continued treating me like garbage and lying to me all the time? He gave me a ring to promise me he would continue breaking my heart

with the same girl or maybe a new one.

I was tired of people coming to me telling me things. I was tired of seeing things on social media. All of that pissed me off so bad. To top it off, he wanted to disrespect me while I was carrying his baby. Nah, I am beyond good. Who would have thought I would hate this man so much? The man I was living with, doing pretty much everything with, messed me up. How could he treat a woman like that when she is pregnant? Sometimes I wish men could carry a baby and see how it feels for real. Watch a video or go in the room when she is about to give birth and tell me how you really feel.

It was time for me to give that up and move on with my life and get away from this crazy man. I finally realized that I was an intelligent, beautiful, talented young lady. I shouldn't let someone treat me like garbage. No one should allow disrespect; I don't care how much love you have for someone. After being hurt so many times, you sit there and think maybe it's you or maybe you're not the one. You haven't thought sometime that relationships just isn't for you anymore? Or one day I will find Mr. Right? Maybe I'll try the relationship thing again further down the line. What is a relationship without trust and communication? Honestly, I thought I found the right one, but I guess not. It was just a dream, I think.

He was different; funny, loving, caring. I thought he was going to be the one for me. One thing I never do is introduce my kids to the guy I am talking to until six months to a year of talking. He was so different, so I introduced him to my kids and family sooner than I should have. Everyone loved him, because he was funny and cool. He was always him and never changed not one bit. He had jokes for days. I would sit there and say to myself, *How does a person have so much energy all day long*? But it was him being him and not putting on a show for anyone.

He was my chocolate king. A man who can cook is an A-plus. He had a lot of things he did not like that I did when we were in a relationship. Did I not mention I was single for a whole four years and probably couple of months? So being in a relationship all over again felt different. I went from being released from a bird cage to being someone's girl. I was not used to telling him, "I'm stepping out," or, "I am home." I went a day without checking on him. Man, I thought I was still living a single life. He was not with it at all. I was playing with a big man's pride.

Things went downhill so fast. We started talking every day on the phone and FaceTime. I thought we were building trust in each other. I had bad trust issues from my previous relationship, so I figured I shouldn't block him out completely. I should try to trust him and open up. I did, but not completely because I was so scared of getting hurt all over again. I was alert about everything with him. We did not spend enough time with each other like I

wanted to and at the same time I thought he was dating someone else and giving her the attention he should have given me. But no, he was going through his problems and I also had problems within myself. So, yeah, we had problems.

After arguing over and over again, I was losing my trust in men. My mind was set on one thing: he has another woman out there who is taking his time. I was so hurt. It really had me in a different set of zones. Even now, it still hurts. I was getting used to him. I hadn't felt that way in a long time. Everyone knew he was the reason I was happy.

Who really wants to start over in a relationship? Not me. I really do not have the time for that. Getting to know someone all over, knowing
what they like from what they don't. Nah, I am good. If we are friends, then okay. If I am talking to someone, I have to trust and believe my partner and hope that he will do the same with me.. It's just the principle of being in a relationship. A lot of people will relate to it and some won't. That is one reason I say a relationship isn't just for me anymore.

I am tired of getting hurt. I am tired of lies. All I ever asked for was time, communication and for someone not to lie to me. I guess I was asking for way too much in the relationship. But doesn't that come with it? I really liked him and thought we would really be together until now. But things happen for a reason.

One thing I also learned is not to involve family and friends in your relationship at all. They will be ones telling you not to talk to a person while they are out there doing the same but ten times worse. Nobody wants to see you happy, just themselves. Sad, but true at the same time. I learned the hard way. If it is really meant to be, then it will be.

You cannot push for something that is not going to happen the second you ask for it.

I really wished it could happen. I missed being held and being told I was beautiful, and how he liked me to be natural. To hear that made me feel like the best woman in the world. Like they say, if it is really meant to be, he will come back. But I will respect his wishes and give him his time. It kind of

works better for me, too, because I can focus on me and getting myself together.

If he really loves you, trust me, it won't go down like that. You guys will find some way to fix things between you, to see if you are willing to continue working on what you started. If he comes back, just hold on to it and make sure you don't make the same mistake again. A lot comes with it, as well. If you are really going through it, once you learn to love yourself, learn what makes you happy first before you try to make someone else happy. I have learned the hard way the route I don't want to go through again.

My past relationship opened my eyes a lot. I know we all have that one relationship that really left some damage inside of us. You will know when it is time to park something and walk away. I waited so many months and years to realize that my son's father was not for me anymore, that he was everyone else's man and that I should not have anybody disrespecting me in any kind of way. I will talk back, whether you like it or not.

I was called a lot of disrespecting things that crushed me. He did not care what he was saying when he was saying it. Not one, "Sorry," have I received until this day. Ask if I would accept it now. Maybe I would, or maybe not. I might accept so he knows how much I've grown up. At the same time, I might not accept it because he violated me so many times and I honestly wouldn't need that sorry. What man really sits there and argues with a female? A man who was not raised right by his mother, that is who. I know if someone was talking to your mother like that you would not like it at all.

I am over it. All my boys are great and doing well. It is sad that their father chooses not to be around because I would not be with him or put up with the mess anymore. But I'm lucky I am who I am today: a strong single mother who doesn't let anything get to her. The most he can say and will say about me is that I am crazy, which is right when it comes to my kids.

People ask, "What about child support?" I get paid more to go to work instead of missing a day to go stand in front of the judge to beg for some money or beg for him to come get his child. I say "beg" because that is exactly what you are doing. He was all with the game having fun until, boom,

you're pregnant. You see how easy that was? So why can't it be so easy for you to come see your child? Why do I have to go to court for you to pro-
vide for your child?

If you are out there living your best life, traveling from right to left and getting money, then put him on child support. But if you are doing it just because he moved on and has another child now,
you need to grow up and get your life together for real. Everyone is different, but that is how I think and see it. I honestly do not have time for court. If he is not working, you are getting $12 a week. My child is worth more than that. But everyone has different cases. I am not bashing anyone, but that is me personally. Some may agree and some may not and that is okay. I am not here to tell you about
yourself. I am not here to judge anyone.

Now, I just enjoy time by traveling with my close friends, turning up every year for my birthday and little girls' night get-togethers. I still remember my birthday in 2018 like It was yesterday. My close co-worker made sure I started off my birthday with a relaxing massage, and then we went out for drinks after. My sisters planned something nice. Even though it didn't go as planned, they still made sure I enjoyed my time.

I lost my first love a couple of months before. I think he's still in jail and he's coming out soon. It still feels unreal to me and to most people. So many times I have said to myself, "Why you? Why did this have to happen to you?" There are so many questions, but one thing I never did was ask God,

"Why you?"

God knew you were stressed out and you still managed to help others, knowing you had your own problems. That is why you were always blessed and still walked around with a smile on your face, because you were so unbothered. I know things happen for a reason, and that is why I cannot be so upset. All I am left with is good memories and I will continue making sure your son, our son, is always

well, all of my boys. I know He's looking down, watching over us saying, "We're good, you're good and you know that." May God bless his soul. We will always miss you and love you Robbie. Please continue watching over your son. You may not be here, but you are here spiritually.

I didn't want to celebrate my birthday at all, but my sisters weren't with it. They made sure I ate before I went out. I got dolled up, and took a couple of shots before we left the house. We arrived at the club, and all my friends were there and my sisters. I was so happy. The bottles kept coming; we all were drinking, dancing and laughing. I had so many bottles coming, people felt our vibes and all the lights were on us. I started feeling tipsy and there

were more bottles coming in. I was worried that I wouldn't be able to walk out. I didn't care. I had my sisters and my close friends. Then I passed out.

The next morning, I woke up with pain all over my body. I had cut my eyebrow, and fractured my wrist and my knee. I was all messed up and hung over, but my friend was hurt, too. The night of my birthday was in the books. All I remember saying was, "If I do, do something for my birthday. I don't want to remember anything for my birthday," which I did not. People told me what happened that night and I thought, "Wow." I do not remember one thing after that.

All I remember is one of my friends saying, "Sip on, girl. It's your birthday," and my sister mixing my drink. I woke up to a locked phone and a lot of messages that I could not access because I locked my phone. My mother was so upset and said she was going to put us all in a rehab. I thought, "Come on, Mom. Talk to me when I am feeling better." I was drinking because of all the stress I had — heartaches, broken pieces, sadness, happiness. I just wanted to have a great night and not come home crying after being drunk.

That does not mean I should continue drinking like that because I am stressed out. It is no excuse for that at all. I am not saying when you are stressed you must drink, but I have experienced, and I was happy I passed out. I just wanted to pass out, so I didn't cry.

I hate crying. I honestly do. Crying takes over my whole body to the point where I do not want to eat. That is no good at all. The question is, do I want to be like that again? No. I hate the hangover feeling, the way my body feels the next day. You cannot eat what you want to eat because you feel like you are coming down with a stomach virus. Everything is just sitting on your chest, and you won't feel any better until you throw up and let it out. Trust me, once everything comes out, that is when you start to feel like yourself again after laying down and drinking plenty of fluid.

I do not know how people can get drunk every day and have that feeling. Some people that drink a lot would say to drink the same thing you had to drink before so you can feel better. I do not believe that at all because I can barely smell liquor after-

ward. It makes me want to throw up even more. You see, after feeling like that, I stay away from liquor for a while. I guess everyone is different on that part, also. That happens occasionally but it is something I cannot do every day. Special days, I would say. Not to get so drunk to the point I do not remember anything, but to have a drink or two, that is all.

Yes, I enjoyed myself, minus the falls that took place after the liquor hit the system, but I can now laugh about it because I am not in pain anymore and my bruises are gone. I still get a pain here and there, but nothing too crazy. I must say that was one of the best birthdays ever. I love you guys. You guys really looked out and made sure I enjoyed myself and made sure I returned to my boys safe and sound.

I am so lucky to have them, I truly am. I know I get on all of their nerves, but it is love. Honestly, if I did not have them there with me, who knows what would have happened to me? I sit there and think about it a lot. You have some "friends" who would leave you there all alone and not care if you reached home or not. These are girls I grew up with and we have a lot of memories we can talk about to this day. These girls are real blood and some became sisters just by earning my trust. My circle will always remain the same, and I do not care how people feel about that. My girls know who they are — no need to write names. They already know how I feel about them, and I know how they feel about me.

I am just living my best life because tomorrow is never promised. Life is so short. You are here today and tomorrow you are gone. That is why I always stay with the I-don't-care feeling on some things. If I said I do not care about anything, then I

would be lying to myself and you guys.

I am very thankful. Imagine if I was out by myself? They made sure I was safe and good and still had a great time. At the same time, I do not want to be that twisted again. I want to remember from beginning to end, not from beginning to the ground, then bed. I have experience a lot so far, so I can put in my book things I have done already.

I tried it once, and that is all I need. I do not want my parents to look at me like I have a drinking problem to the point where I cannot control it and they must worry every second. If you cannot control yourself, then you should not be drinking at all. You may go out with different sets of friends, and you never know if they would have to leave early or care how you get home after. That is true.

You should know your limit, but as you all know I was celebrating my birthday and dealing with a loss at the same time. That is still not an excuse. I am just saying, though, that is what happens when you mix Henny with champagne. Never again will

I do that. Lesson learned. That is a bad, dangerous move right there.

I've been through so many things, but losing someone you were close to and had a child with is the hardest thing to get over. Mind you, I still have unanswered questions about why I have so much
anger inside of me. Instead of trying to figure it out, I'm still adding more to the plate and I'm still left with unanswered questions.

Yes, now I am even angrier because you are no longer here. I am here, raising all my boys by myself.
You know he liked it when you guys went shopping together. When he was going through something, he ran to you. When I try to help, he always tells me it is not the same. I cannot be mommy and daddy. It hurts so badly. Sometimes I sit there and think if I pushed harder, maybe you could have changed, and we would have worked on things like we said we would. I know you had your own things going on. I wish I could have

done something then. I know you are still with me, watching over us. I truly miss you, always and forever.

I think to myself every day that there so many opportunities out there, but I am too scared to make a move because I do not know if someone is going to turn me down. It happens all the time, to the point I get sick to my stomach. Once I go to try it out, then I am fine once I hear good news. I can interview someone and train someone, but I do not like it when it is done to me. I guess that is the boss mind thinking already. I always get nervous; I do not know why I do.

I am always thinking negatively. One thing I know is that if you are always thinking negatively, negative things are always going to happen. That happens a lot of the time. When you think too much on something, it does not come out right, especially if you are trying to do more than one thing at a time. If you put your mind to it, then you shall achieve it. That is why I stay positive

now and will remind myself, too. If I was not staying positive I probably
would not reach this far at all.

I thank that man above all. So many times he heard me crying, wiped my tears and told me to get myself together. Guess what? That is exactly
what I am doing now. Whenever I am stressing, I tend to put it in writing. That is how I release my stress. It really helps me a whole lot. I would rather write than talk, if you ask me. I can always go back and read and compare my blessings. Some people who stress tend to pick up a drinking habit and guess what that causes? It causes fights, arguments, etc. Stress drinking can cause a lot of bad things. I should say, all types of different stress can cause a lot of damage without you knowing
it, before it is too late. There are people who block themselves off from people until they get themselves back together.

Everyone acts differently when it comes to stress. Me, I start thinking of so many things to do at one time and guess what happens? I get too overwhelmed and leave everything alone. I found my comfort zone, which is writing. I never knew writing could be so enjoyable. Writing makes me feel so relaxed that I block everything out, and I mean everything. I even block out my boys just to write and clear my head at times. Find something that makes you comfortable and stress-free and go for it.

I notice when I keep everything in, I get so stressed and so upset. All I used to do was lock myself in my room, stay in my car for an hour just to think or even take a hot, long shower, just have the hot water running down my back and release the stress. If you cannot control your own stress, then it is best to seek help. Stress can make a big impact on your life. Stress can make you do crazy things and kill you. Play if you want. Sometimes you can do other things to get your mind off a lot of worries if you put your mind to it. Believe in yourself, and always put yourself first. Nobody else will.

Every day, I sit and listen to everyone's stories. There are a lot of people who are dealing with worse things you cannot compare to at all. The most you can do is give some advice, hoping it will help them further down the line and continue to pray for them, because you want the best for them as well. A lot people say I should consider helping others on the side which I do not mind, but I want to fix me first before I worry about someone else. How can I tell another to fix themselves when I am not completely there yet myself? That would be me talking just to talk and honestly, I do not have the time for that at all.

If I am talking to you and giving you advice, I would like it if you would really listen and take what I am saying seriously. Run with it, try it out, and see how it works. Thank me later when you have done it. Now, you have the girls who will ask you a question, then some advice on how they should go about something, but they are still on the first line. The second time, I answer the question in a different way and tell them how they should go about it in the same way, but they still have not made a move because they are too scared. Why are

you scared? If you continue allowing certain things, then certain things are going to continue to happen. Either you want change, or you do not. You still want to ask questions and not do anything about it.

I don't know. The way my mind is set, I'm searching things on my own, talking to older people, and learning new things I never knew. The number of things I know for my age, you would have thought I was way older or had definitely been through worse. Nope, it's just me wanting to know more things, meet more people, and learn new things. There's nothing wrong with that all.

I love to learn new things. The things I've learned can help another out there. Maybe I can teach single mothers like me things that half of them do not know right now because they are too busy depending on people. That is one thing you cannot do. Make your own, learn new things, flip, keep that pattern in mind.

When it comes to my boys, I cannot depend on anyone. Yes, I have help if needed, but I will reach out when that day comes, God forbid. Until then, I

will continue doing my best with my boys. My life isn't perfect, and I'm not rich either. I have days when I am struggling but it's normal; it can happen to anyone. I will never show my kids I am struggling. I deal with that alone. I do not want them

worrying about anything but school and each other.

Staying in a house, apartment, or room wherever is not good, either. You start to think of everything that you could have accomplished in life or about life, period. Trust me, I get tired of thinking.

I just want to move around and do things so I won't think too much. Thinking too much makes your head start to hurt and when that starts to happen you cannot even focus right. I think a lot. I think too much because there are so many things I must still accomplish from my list to feel fully completed. If

you are thinking, put it down in writing. Get some things off your mind. Make space so you can still remember things you were just talking about five minutes ago. Do not get me wrong. Sometimes you have to sit there and think about your life and how you can make things better, or even make a right move, just think, or whatever. It may be happy or sad.

Have fun, travel, do whatever makes you happy. Do not sit and wait on happiness; it won't just come like that. Ask yourself in the mirror, "Who's that person? Do I know who she is?? If you can answer those questions with your head up high, well, pat yourself in the back. A lot of people cannot answer them, and I was one of those people.

I was running and looking for happiness when I did not know who Janny was to begin with.

Stress can have a big and I mean impact on your life — trust and believe that. Stress can come at anytime, anywhere. Think about yourself first and what makes you happy at all times, before you go out there trying to make someone else happy who isn't happy

with themselves. Stress made me do things I did not want to do. Being stressed all the time and trying to make others happy isn't the answer, either.

I'm the type of person who makes sure everyone around me is always taken care of before I am. I always want to see others happy. There are a lot of selfish people out there who are always looking for help, but when you are in need of a return favor there are always excuses.

Lucky thing I am not the type to depend on anyone. If I do not have it I always figure out a plan, which works about 97.5 percent of the time. The way I am, even if I am struggling I won't show it, or I won't ask for help unless it's a close friend of mine and I don't even like doing that most of the time. People love to throw a lot of what they did for

you in your in face and I definitely don't have the time for that. Let me remind you that I am hot-tempered and don't care what comes out at the time. So

yeah, I guess you get it now.

I hate embarrassment and I hate for people to walk around and talk about me because of money. If I borrow something, I will let you know when I am going to give it back, date and time. I work hard for my own things. The way people are these days, I would rather struggle with the little change I have instead of asking to borrow money from someone that will end up talking about you and what they have done for you. Everyone is so different. If I have it and a family member or friend of mine asks to borrow something, trust and believe I will give it. God will always bless me in many different ways. That is how I look at things.

That right there messed me up completely. I'm so used to being Superwoman and the "yes man" to everything. When it's time to say no, it is so hard for me to get the word out my mouth, I feel so bad. But if you think about it, do you think the other person would feel bad for saying no? Half of the time, they don't. They will bring up a bunch of reasons for why they cannot do it or whatever. Nobody can make you do something you do not want to do, period.

For me to be unstressed, I have to focus on myself first. I have to think about what I need to complete myself before I worry about someone else. I hear this all the time, "Stop putting yourself last. Once you are good, then you can worry about everyone else." This is definitely true if everyone else is only thinking about themselves. The type of person I am, I will stop what I am doing to help someone else with their problems and not think that I have my own problems to handle, as well. That is so stressful, and I get so overwhelmed. Honestly, I'm so fed up and tired of it. It's time for me to put my thinking hat back on, snap back into the light and ask myself what I am doing.

All of this stress came from a lot of places, I think. From my parents not letting us go out and hang with friends, and only playing in the backyard with my sisters and brothers. The only time we got to explore outside was going to school. My parents said the safe place was home, there were so many crazy people out there. So I was going to enjoy every freed time I got, because once I went back home that was it. There was no going back out unless it was with my parents or a family member.

Yes, I was mad at my parents because they wouldn't let us go to friends' houses. Like Caribbean parents say, "Your friend is home. Your friend is us," meaning family. So I stopped asking. Being locked in a house was not cool, but if you ask me if I am still upset about my parents not letting me out the house, my answer will be, "No." I am the same parent now. My kids are not allowed to go to friends' houses every day; maybe once or twice a week. I will not have my kids running the streets like they do not have no home, but I am not going to keep them in the house like my parents did to us. I want them to do things that I was not able to do as a child. I want them to have a better life than I did. I want to see them do well; chart the path and not follow friends. I want them to be the leaders, not the followers.

I know my parents were always like that. They just wanted the best for all of us. My mom hates kids that roam the street or get into trouble being at the wrong place at the wrong time. I hate it when she repeats the same line all the time. Maybe that is why I am who I am with my boys. It could be. I will not be that strict mom, but I am not a pushover, either. There is nothing wrong with saying *no* to going outside. They will call me mean. It's okay. I can be mean. They are going to be mad for that second and then forget about it and find something else to do with their time.

I see a lot of kids who don't respect their parents and do what they want, when they want.

That is one thing I will not accept, period. My boys know when to act up and they know when I am serious. I don't believe in beating a kid; I really don't. My kids know when they do something bad, I get upset. It is how you raise your kid. They know their limits on what not to do. My boys are different in their own ways. They all love to joke, just like their mommy. I wouldn't change them for anything in the world.

So many things are happening in this cold world we live in today. If it's not being hated, it is having a fake friend, a friend who wants everything you have or just wants to be you. As a parent, I think about all of that because when I was growing up I went through all of that. I was bullied, talked about, almost jumped, etc. Now that I am grown up I changed a lot, but just don't get on my bad side. Imagine your child. I would lose my mind.

My boys are my weakness. Say their names, touch them, whatever it is, I will block out, period. No talking. That is why I have talks with my boys all the time. I will tell them something, then give explanations, too. I know they hate it when I talk all the time, but oh well. My mom did it to me, and I have my boys to talk to now. It's life. You are going to hear things you already know. I just want it glued to your head.

If it's not people kidnapping to make money, it's someone hating because you are getting money.

The list goes on. That is why I always tell my boys,

"You do not need so many friends. You do not need friends to be cool. You guys can be cool by yourselves, if you ask me. There are three of you guys.

You all have me and each other. That's a perfect team right there." You know that is not what they want to hear.

Just sit there and watch. There are some many signs right in front of you, but you are too blind to see it. So many things happened to me, but me being so hard-headed I may do it again, or something else that is similar. So many times I almost lost my life over partying, so I put that to rest. My life is way too important for that and I am a mother to three

wonderful, handsome boys who need their mother.

Now that I am getting older, I know what I want to accomplish in life and what I am looking for. I

write down what I want to accomplish on a piece of paper. When I achieve my goals, I cross them out. It motivates you to keep going. Have you ever looked at something and said you cannot do it?

Yeah, that is me all the time. I always say I cannot do something, then I try it and guess what happens? I did not believe in myself and I did something I thought I couldn't do. I go for what I always wanted to do with nobody stopping me.

All I need is one sign to trust and believe and I will never do it again because my boys need me, and I need them. Some people are just too hardheaded. Once they get a sign, they don't care and they continue doing the same thing all over again. Do not wait until it's too late to fix something that could have been fixed. Remember that. Sad, but true. There are a lot of people who don't care about life and what they do and how dangerous a situation may be. Once you get a little blessing, take it and be happy. Never be too greedy in the game. I do not need to explain this part; you know what I am talking about. Think smart.

Do not wait on anyone to help you fix yourself, either. That same person you are waiting on might have his or her own problems as well and won't be able to take on another load. By waiting, you are pushing your dreams back just because you are too afraid to face your own troubles. The longer you

wait, the longer it takes. Think about it.

If you were struggling and you knew someone who was struggling as well, would you put your dreams aside to satisfy another? There are those who will. Honestly, I am well used to being that person. I am getting older, not younger. There's not much I can give but some advice that I hope will help in the long run. I am hoping you will take my

word and run with it and see if it works. Not a lot of people will like that, but that's all you can really do at the time.

One thing I've noticed, and I've seen it done a lot of times, is that people are willing to put themselves last to help someone else. Yes, that is very true, because I am that person with the soft heart. Ask me if that is helping me in the long run? No, it is not, because I am always making sure everyone around me is all right before I focus back on me,

which isn't good at all. There are so many things I could have accomplished, some of my goals, if I had put my all into it. But no more waiting. It's time to get back to me and worry about myself first before I worry about someone else and their problems that they are not trying to fix.

It is never too late to accomplish your goals. Age is just a number. People older than us are still going to school, working, modeling, acting, writing, you name it. They are just trying to make a living that will last a lifetime. It takes the amount of time you put in to reach that goal, because no one is going to complete your work for you. If you have that support team, by all means take it. Do not let that good thing slide by. You will be happy in the long run and will be telling people your story about how you accomplished those goals of yours. They will be the first ones in the front of the line screaming your name, that same support team. You did it. Never bite the hands that feed you.

That does not mean I am not going to help others, either. I know my words will help others out there who feel like they cannot accomplish anything in life because they are single parents, have no family, have no job, or whatever the cause maybe. No, I never said I will never help another again, but one thing I'm saying is that I am going to put myself first at all times. No more putting other peoples' problems before mine. Are you going to continue doing that the rest of your life? Why continue doing it for someone who isn't trying on their own? Are you planning to do this forever? Sometimes you must let them learn on their own. If they didn't have you, how would they have done it? They

would have figured out a plan, right? With this type of heart, I have I cannot see myself saying *no* to someone who needs my help. If I see you making time for other things than your problem, well then, I am sorry you have to learn how it really is out here and realize you cannot always depend on people.

Maybe that is why they take advantage of me. Who knows? Maybe they know me too well and they know I am not going to say *no*. I may take my time to answer, but my answer is always *yes*. If I really don't have it, I will answer sooner than you know it, "Not at this time." Maybe I do not like to be the mean person. Who knows? Trust and believe that I am so fed up and tired of it now. I am so used to helping out everyone with their problems that I even forget about my own. That is really sad. If only I was like them, but I am not. I will never change who I am as a person, but I will not allow someone to come in and use me for the little I have

worked for by myself.

Look at me. I am not perfect; nobody is. It is how you push yourself out there. I am a single parent to three wonderful boys. Yes, I have my days when I feel like I'm all alone with no help, I get stressed out and I cry to myself, but that does not mean it is the end of the world. That is just me saying I need to push a little harder. My time will soon come when I won't need to struggle anymore and my tears will turn to happy tears. I look at myself in the mirror every day and tell myself each and every day, "I am strong. I can do this with just a push." God would not give me anything I cannot manage. I reach too far to accomplish some of my goals to turn around and leave with nothing at the end. One day at a time and one thing at a time. No rush.

A lot people look at me and say I make it look so easy being a single mother. I always walk the streets with my head up, always smiling. No, it is not easy being a single mother to three kids. I break down when the load on my back gets too heavy for me to carry, but that's not the end of the world. It may sound easy, but it is not. Try coming home from work, and checking all three kids' homework, making sure they eat dinner, shower, take out clothes for school the next day, and the list goes on. Do that every day, seven days a week, twenty-four hours, non-stop. Your job as a mother never ends.

I shouldn't be as mad and stressed as I am because I went looking for it. I am not going to just leave my boys out there and think someone is going to take care of my boys for me. Definitely not. Being a single parent comes with a lot of work.

Yes, I am going to walk with my head up, because I know I am doing a great job taking care of boys.

I know what I have and what I have to do to make sure my boys are taken care of and set for life. Yes, I have to walk with my head up. I am not here to play anymore. I'm here to accomplish my goals. Yes, I'm always smiling. Why should I be mad? Why should I walk around mad at the world? The world did not get me pregnant. The world did not give me my problems or stress. Be mad at yourself. My problems stay home where they belong. I do not carry that load with me wherever I go. Who wants to be around someone who

is always complaining about problems? Not me. That brings too much negativity around and they don't realize that. Do something about it so you can stop complaining and stressing. All of that time you take out just to complain about something, is the same time you could have been using to fix it. Do people really think when they are talking? I don't think so... They are wasting a lot of time. I am not a tape recorder. I am not going to keep repeating myself. Sorry, but I am not.

If people would leave their problems at home, we probably would not have so many mad people walking around blaming everyone else for their problems, or walking around getting mad at every little thing when they should be happy. When I'm mad, it brings out a different me that I hate seeing. I know I am not that person. I know I am way better than that.

With the kind of job I do, I love helping people in need. I work in the healthcare field and you meet mean, nice, and rude people every day. You say to
yourself, "I hope when I get old I am not that angry." Those are people who have problems of their own and just feel it is okay to take it out on you. So,

what you do in return? The same thing, right? I smile back, to show them that I am not going to let their miserable behinds mess up my day. I say, "Hope you have a blessed day," close the door and walk out. There are times and places for that.

When I am upset, I walk around and cool off in the corner. I can easily tell you about yourself, but sometimes that isn't worth it either, arguing with someone who isn't on your level, who is so upset that she can walk around mad at the world for her problems. Go drink a cup of tea. You will be right all right, sis. People like that do not get any attention from me and do not deserve any, either. The best way to ignore them is to kill them with your kindness.

Every day, I thank God for everything He has done for me. There have been a lot of rocky roads, but I know they can be fixed if I do it and don't just sit around thinking it is going to just happen by itself. I came a long way from being pregnant at an early age, finishing school, getting money, and taking care of my boys all by myself. If I can do it, I know a lot of people can. It may sound easy, but it is not. It takes a lot of effort. I know I wouldn't have made it this far without pushing myself more, or without my family and friends by my side.

I can say that when I'm up to doing something, everyone is happy for me and pushes me even more to do what I want. Who knows? A bigger door may open for me down the line, but I'm still trying other things as well. That is the type of vibe you need around you at all time. If it isn't #teamJay, then I do not need you around me with your negativity.

Keep that in mind. We are all here to win and make big moves in life.

I had stress after stress because I could not do what normal kids do. My mother was always hard on me on all sides, like how we carried ourselves, finishing school, etc. My mother would always say, "I want my kids to have businesses, finish school, get a degree, get married, have kids, drive nice cars and live in a big house." Yeah, that is everyone's dream, Mom. At least, that's every parent's dream for their kids. Every day, my mother would give us that talk. I get it. She wants the best for all us. She

wants us to follow our dreams and stick to them.

One thing with my mother is that she will make sure all of her kids are okay, and even our close friends. That is one of the things I like about my mommy. My dad is the same way but a more chill dude and he loves to crack jokes on people. If you tell him what you want to do, and you do it, he will be the one waiting until you get home to ask how everything went and tell you, "I told you were going to get it. See?" I love my parents. They are my biggest support team ever, even though they drive me crazy.

My mother's main problem is seeing us with different men in our lives. "Why can't you guys settle down and find someone to spend the rest of your life with?" It will happen when it is the right time. I wish it was that easy, the way you made it sound, Mom. I am tired of looking for the right one. They always say, "Wait and the right one will come." I guess. I waited a long time and one came.

Every time I think I found the right one, I am wrong. Either they are not ready to settle down or they lead me to liking them too much and getting hurt, whatever the case may be at the time. Now I just look at relationships as a play thing because I do not know if it is long-term thing or not. Come on now, we hear this all the time. No parent wants to meet a different man every six months to a year, or maybe more often. It does not look good at all.

The way you carry yourself is how they are going to treat you, period. That is one thing I've noticed. Sometimes things do not go well between you and your partner, so you just let them go and stay single until you are ready to date again. Or you
just stay single, focusing on yourself and patiently waiting for your time to come.

At this point, I have given up on looking for the right one and waiting for the right one. Maybe relationships aren't for me at all, because my partner and I might want different things. Yes, I would like to be in a relationship further down the road, get married and have my own family one day, if God's

willing. Being in a relationship comes with a lot of things like trust and communication. Without those key things, your relationship will not work. There cannot be just one person in the relationship who

is willing to work things out. It has to be both of you guys working together as a team. No team, no relationship.

You cannot depend on people voting for your own relationship to work when deep down you know that you and your partner cannot fix the problem between you. You have to make the time for each to make each other happy and not distance yourselves from each other. If you are willing to distance yourself, you might as well call it quits.

There is no taking breaks when you feel like it — do that on your own time, by yourself. You are not hurting yourself because you choose to do that; you are hurting the other one who is willing to spend time with you and put their all into you. Some people do not think when it comes to things like this. Stop being selfish now. Treat others how you
want to be treated.

Some might say I'm wrong, and some may agree with me. Everyone looks at relationships differently. The way I look at relationships, you must have trust. If there's no trust then you guys should not be together, because there will be a lot of disagreements. If there is no communication, you are going to think your partner is hiding things from
you, period. I do not care what anyone says.

You have to spend time with each other. It doesn't matter where you guys go, as long you see him. Hearing from him does not mean you guys have to be on the phone twenty-four hours a day, but a message here and there checking to see how

you are doing or you checking on him, making sure his day is going well. That would be nice. Am I

wrong? Is that too much to ask for? It is just the simplest thing.

Here is the problem. When you start moving differently and writing when you feel like it, they don't like that. That is when they start to think if you are speaking to someone else. I tell you, the guilt is so real. That is not the only sad part. They will act all big and all, like they don't need you, and leave you alone. Months later, you will get messages, phone calls and all. That is so funny to me. Back then he didn't want me because he was too cool for me, and he had all types hitting him up. Now he wants me to come back? He must think I'm his yo-yo or something, so you can roll me out and roll me back up when he feels like it.

Now I am moving on to bigger and better things. If he did that to me once, he can always do it again but ten times worse. Sorry, but not sorry.

It would be nice to walk around knowing I have that one person I can go home to and cuddle and spend some time with. Go out and have some fun here and there. You do not have to go out every time to have fun with your partner. Sometimes seeing him or being around him brings you joy.

If Mr. Right comes, I will just take it slow and try not to let what I have been through block me from being me. That, in itself, can mess up a relationship. If you have been through so much of giving your all in every relationship and all you get at the end is a broken heart, you get your mind set on not letting the next person do it to you again. But when you are all caught up in the relationship, you are too blind to see what is going on in front of you. By the time you have come to your senses, it is already too late. I know some can relate to this, but life goes on. Either you are in love or you are

just tired of the games and all.

I just want to be happy and loved. I want to be able to walk around and say, "I have a man," with a big smile on my face. Who doesn't want this, minus the stress and arguments that come along

with it? I would take happiness over stress any day, if you ask me.

My problem is that I am too scared of getting my heart broken. I am scared to give my all in a relationship. I am scared to start all over in a relationship because I don't know if it is real. That is where I am wrong. I can have Mr. Right in front of me, but just because I am scared of getting my heart broken I block a lot of things out, like my feelings. It's hard for me to express my feelings. If I do express my feelings, I do not know if I am going to chase him away or not. I do not know how he is going to think of me after. There are a lot of things I think about. I don't know if it is a good thing or not.

Honestly, that is why I move like a dude most of the time. The way they treat some females, I feel it's only right to play their own cards on them, but that is when they get mad and don't like it. I figured if I did that, maybe it would change them a little or they would see how it feels to get hurt. Am I the only one who thinks like this? I hear it all the time:

I move like a dude. "Stop acting like a dude. You're a female. You cannot do what they do, so stop it." I thought about it. My mind is like a dude. I am tired of getting hurt.

Who isn't tired of getting hurt? If you are treating your partner right, it is only right if he does the same in return. Let me know if I'm wrong. All we want is honestly, communication, and time. Am I the only one who is thinking about this? Let me know what

you are looking for. Is that too much to ask?

Maybe that is why I do not trust anymore. Who knows? Trust is the main problem I know I have. If I cannot trust you, I don't want you, period. If you are out working, hanging with friends, or whatever you are doing, and I do not trust you, then your communication sucks. Each person may have his or her own opinion. That is how I think and see things because I have trust issues. If communication was on point, maybe you could look at things differently.

After being hurt over and over again, who would honestly be able to trust again? You start to think everyone else is going to do the same thing. All of your hopes are out the window. That is why I choose not to date anymore. Maybe one day I will meet Mr. Right. Who knows? As for now, being single is perfect for me, in a way. No stress, no telling the other where you go and going out when
you please.

Honestly, I think I'm over relationships, period. After my first true love, who I had my first born with, I did not think I could love another. Years later, I decided maybe I should give it a try again,

which I did. This went on for years and I thought it was actually going somewhere. I was happy until things started going wrong. Lies started and my trust was not there anymore. Imagine living with someone, going everywhere together, being on the phone with each other when you're both at work, then, boom! You get a phone call saying that your partner is out there, cheating.

What would be your first reaction? Every girl's reaction is to flip out. That is what I did. Maybe if I had not flipped, I would have known sooner that my partner really was cheating and the times he said he was at work, he really was not. Maybe if I had not flipped, I would have known sooner that she

was also carrying a baby for him, as well. So many maybes, right? What I should have done was play it cool (that's coming from a hot head). If I played it cool the whole time and listened to what people were telling me, I would have caught him a long time before and gone about my business.

Instead, I flipped out and he still lied, but he was alert now. He knew I had no proof of what I was saying. I dug until I found out the truth, and his other woman was digging, too. She called me and told me everything and what did he do? Continue to lie to my face. My trust was halfway gone by then. This was someone I chose to stay with, someone my family loved, someone I trusted around my boys, someone I was living with, someone I shared everything with.

I was broken into pieces. My trust was completely gone. I did not feel like myself at all. I felt like a piece of me was missing. Let me re-word that:
He had me walking around looking dumb. People would see me and him, and then see him and her. Get it? The dude played his cards right for a long time. He was living two lifestyles. He was living his best life until he got caught in his own games.

I hear girls with their stories about how their man cheated on them but they still love them. I get it. You are in love and you feel he's the only one in the world for you.

You are wrong. They will say the most to you, call you fat, ugly, call out your name, or say nobody

will want you because you have kids. That is not true. Yes, I was told all of that. I did not care anymore. I let myself go. I did not dress up because in my head I thought I was fat and nobody was going to talk to me. Many times, I felt ugly even when I did dress up. I went into depression, stayed in the house and did not go out at all because of what this guy put in my head. After months of depression crying pretty much every night, I knew it was not healthy at all. I went from not eating to gaining a lot of weight.

One day I looked at myself in the mirror and said it was time for a change. I am strong and pretty. Do not let anybody take that away from you. I will not let anybody put me down at all, making me feel so uncomfortable in my own skin. When I tell you he damaged me — my soul, my mind — it was not a joke at all. He really had me thinking that nobody would really want me. That school is for dumb people.

With God's strength and praying that I would get through this, I managed to stand with my head up and kill him with my words. I had the support of my family and friends. I felt like a bird that had been released from a cage. That felt so good. That was the day I made a complete change in my life.

I went from being in a relationship to being stalked by my partner, cheated on, lied to, and treated like trash just because I did not want to be with him anymore. I chose happiness over stress, but I did not let that stop me. I had to find myself after being locked in a relationship that I thought was going to last a lifetime.

One thing I learned from this relationship was that he had changed me into a monster. We argued every day, which was not healthy. People who are not happy with themselves are not going to want to see you happy. People who are jealous can hurt you — maybe kill you, too. A person who is out there cheating will continue to blame you for what they are out there doing.

Some people feel that if they partner is jealous it is cute. It is a little cute until the crazy side starts to show, until that partner starts stalking you and watching you through your window at night. That is scary. There's nothing cute about that at all. Like when you go out with friends and ignore your partner and you get a text, "I know you see me calling. I saw you get in the car." Then you look back and forth, side to side, thinking, *Where is this man hiding?* I have been through it all. I do not know how some people live in that lifestyle, or should I say *like* that type of lifestyle.

Who am I to judge? I was once that person who was dealing with it for four years and changed. I was judged. A lot of people had so much to say. Ask me if I cared what other people were saying. No, I did not. They always say it is not good to listen to other people, especially if their relationship isn't perfect. If you don't have a man, why are you talking? It is always good to make your own decisions. Do not get me wrong. Sometimes your

friends or family might give you some good advice, but sometimes it's best to keep certain comments to yourself.

I knew it was time to walk away. I did not want to deal with the stress anymore. I missed myself. I needed this block to move out of my life. Once I did that, all doors were opening. So many blessings came while I was by myself. What does that tell you? He did not want me to be happy at all. He

wanted me to be the person he wanted me to be, which is *nobody*.

I had to catch myself really quick and snap back to reality. Who wants to go through that? Love is love, but trust is another thing. Without trust, there is nothing. Trust is the main key in a relationship, then comes communication. Without those, you might as well stay by yourself, point blank.

Some people feel they must have someone to, have fun, to travel, etc. You do not. That is why people make the dumbest mistake ever. Get to know yourself first. Trust yourself first, love yourself first. Do not put anybody ahead of yourself. If you cannot turn up on your own, how do you think it's going to happen when you are in a relationship?

If you are unhappy with something, speak up. Nobody is a mind reader. Like they say, a closed mouth doesn't get fed. Holding back how you really feel makes you move differently in a relationship. It will have you second-guessing if you really want to be in the relationship or not. Should you stay single the rest of your life?

After what I have been through, it is hard for me to trust another person. I will always have my guard up at all times to protect myself from getting hurt again. That's me, personally. It is not good to do so, because who knows? The next person could be the one you have been asking for, but because you know what you have been through you automatically think he's going to do the same thing to you.

Not everyone is the same. You might find that one person who truly cares about you and shows you things you did not know. He might teach you new things. You never know what can happen if you just try and take it slow. Don't block someone else who is actually trying to be there for you because you are scared of what is going to happen.

That is one of my problems. I am scared to give my all and get hurt again. I do not want that feeling again. Yeah, all relationships have ups and down. No relationships is perfect. I feel that is how you really get to know that person.

Every day I meet a lot of people. Hearing their stories, I sit there and say, "And this whole time I thought mine was really bad." People have it really bad out there, but they are still trying something to make it in life and better themselves.

My whole purpose for writing is to let people know that they are not the only ones who are going through things in life. Look at me and my problems:

Many sleepless nights, stressful nights, etc. I won't let any of that stop me from achieving my dreams. I

waited way too long now to reach this far. Believe in yourself. Trust yourself first before you go trusting somebody else. Other people have it worse than us, but some still manage to keep going.

We are living in a cold world. You see someone today and tomorrow they are gone. That is why I tell my kids I love them every day. I am letting all the single parents know, just because you had a baby at an early age does not mean you cannot accomplish your goals in life. Yes, there may be a lot of rocky roads down the line, but it is never too late to accomplish your dreams.

Age is just a number. Yes, it takes time to do, but are you willing to put some time aside to accomplish what you really want to do? Only you can answer that. No one else can. Whatever you put your mind to, do it. Remember, there are always going to be one or two people telling you, you cannot do it. Do not listen to them. Ask them what they accomplished in life. Ninety-nine percent of the time it is nothing. So keep your comments to

yourself, please and thank you.

Nobody is perfect in life, not even me, but one thing I know is I am going for what is mine. I am doing everything I always wanted to do, which is writing (I picked that up two and a half years ago) and modeling and plenty more to come. I am trying and doing everything. One of them, or maybe all, might work out in the long run.

You come first at all times. If you are not happy, then you cannot make anyone happy, period. That is how people end up with broken hearts and people try to explain something that just cannot be explained, period. There are certain things that can be addressed and certain things you just walk away from because you do not want to hear the same lame excuses for the reason why they did

you wrong.

If you love the person like you said you did, why continue hurting them, whether you guys are in a relationship or not? The person still can get hurt if you guys are only broken up for a month or whatever time it may be. That is what I do not get. If it was the other way around, 99.9% of the time he would tell you to leave him alone because you are the worst person ever. So why can't it go for us females as well? You did wrong. Just let her go and follow her wishes. If anything, it was best to leave the person alone instead of leading him back to something that can never be fixed. If you love the person, don't you want to work things out first before you go doing your dirt? If you love the person, don't you want to see them happy? Before you go and do your stupid stuff, you should have thought about how it can really hurt the person so badly that they don't want to see or speak to you anymore.

Trust me when I say I have no more trust left inside of me anymore. I am broken into pieces that I don't think anyone else will be able to fix because I honestly won't let them. If only if he knew how much I really cared about him, who knows? Maybe he wouldn't have treated me the way he did. All of these lame excuses just pissed me off even more, telling me I don't understand when there is really nothing there to understand. If you messed up big time, tell me how you can explain that situation? Like I said, some can be explained and some just cannot, especially if I heard it already.

It just doesn't make any type of sense at all. You sound really stupid right now. Put your feet in my shoes and tell me how you would feel. You were in a relationship with someone for a couple of months, you guys had some issues, you break up and boom – he has another relationship. Not to mention that he is going through so much that being in a relationship isn't the right thing for him right now and that he needs to work on him and whatever the story may be.

Honestly. Hearing that, what would you do? How do you accept this type of treatment? I just cannot accept it. You feel it is okay to treat anyone like that and it is not cool. You are messing with people's feelings and hurting them so badly, then you think you guys can just come to an understanding and be friends. Oh no. What world do you come from? It must be a world of I-don't-care-how-you-feel.

That whole line of, "Maybe in the future we will be line;" I do not like it and do not want to hear that line again. It was all a dream the whole time.

You had me thinking we really had something good going on. You lied to me big time, when only all I ever lied about was very small and you still flipped out. All you did was tell me about myself pretty much all the time, telling people all I did was stress you out, when deep down you were stressing yourself out about something you could have fixed.

We have some ungrateful people out there, we do. All they do is think about themselves and nobody else. I could go on for days, but at this time I am worried about me and only me. I hope you are happy now. P.S., you did this, not I. I learned that in a hard way. Ask yourself in the mirror, "Who is this person?" What are your goals? Are you ready to take what belongs to you? Are you ready to accomplish those long-term goals of yours? Do you love yourself? Do you really know who you are? Do you deserve to get treated like garbage? There are so many questions you can ask yourself.

My name is Janny Bonhomme and I also go by Jayjay. My goals are to finish my book and become one of the top bestsellers, get a big house, get married, and become rich. At least have enough money to last a lifetime. I want to flip and open up businesses.

Yes, I am ready. I pushed my dreams aside so many times to make others happy. I am so ready. If

you only knew how ready I was a long time ago. No more playing. Yes, I love myself. Yes, after all these

years I finally know who I really am.

I am a young mother of three wonderful boys. I am a loving, caring, down–to-earth, intelligent young lady who loves who she is. Guess what? I got accepted to a modeling agency. This is just the beginning of my dreams and accomplishing my goals. I am beyond happy right now. If you only knew. There are many more to come, just watch. I

will keep you guys posted.

To be continued...

76

About The Author

Janny Bonhomme was born January 19,1990 in Queens NY. She grew up in Rosedale, where she and her siblings were raised. She wrote her first book at the age of 26 years old, but did not think of getting it published and putting it out there to the world. The idea of writing an autobiography about herself was written based on a series of major events that have occurred in her life which have shaped her to be the woman she is today. In this book, you will learn the major events that occurred and how she overcome them. We hope this book can influence not only grown women but young women as well.

follow me on ig @ Janny Bonhomme

P.s please leave a review on amazon.